Loon Chase

With best wishes!

Written by Jean Heilprin Diehl   Illustrated by Kathryn Freeman

This book is dedicated to the memory of Miles—JHD & KF
The author and illustrator donate a portion of their royalties to the
Loon Preservation Committee (www.loon.org).
Thanks to Harry Vogel (LPC) and to the staff of the
Maine Audubon for reviewing the
"For Creative Minds" section and verifying its accuracy.

ISBN 13: 978-0-9764943-8-6
ISBN 10: 0-9764943-8-8
Library of Congress Control Number: 2005931000

Sylvan Dell Publishing
976 Houston Northcutt Blvd., Suite 3
Mt. Pleasant, SC 29464

www.SylvanDellPublishing.com
copyright permission: copyright@SylvanDellPublishing.com

Early one summer morning, before breakfast, Mom and I paddled to Big Island to pick blueberries. Our dog, Miles, leaped off the dock to swim with us. His nose puffed just above the water: pfuh-huh, pfuh-huh – pfuh-huh.

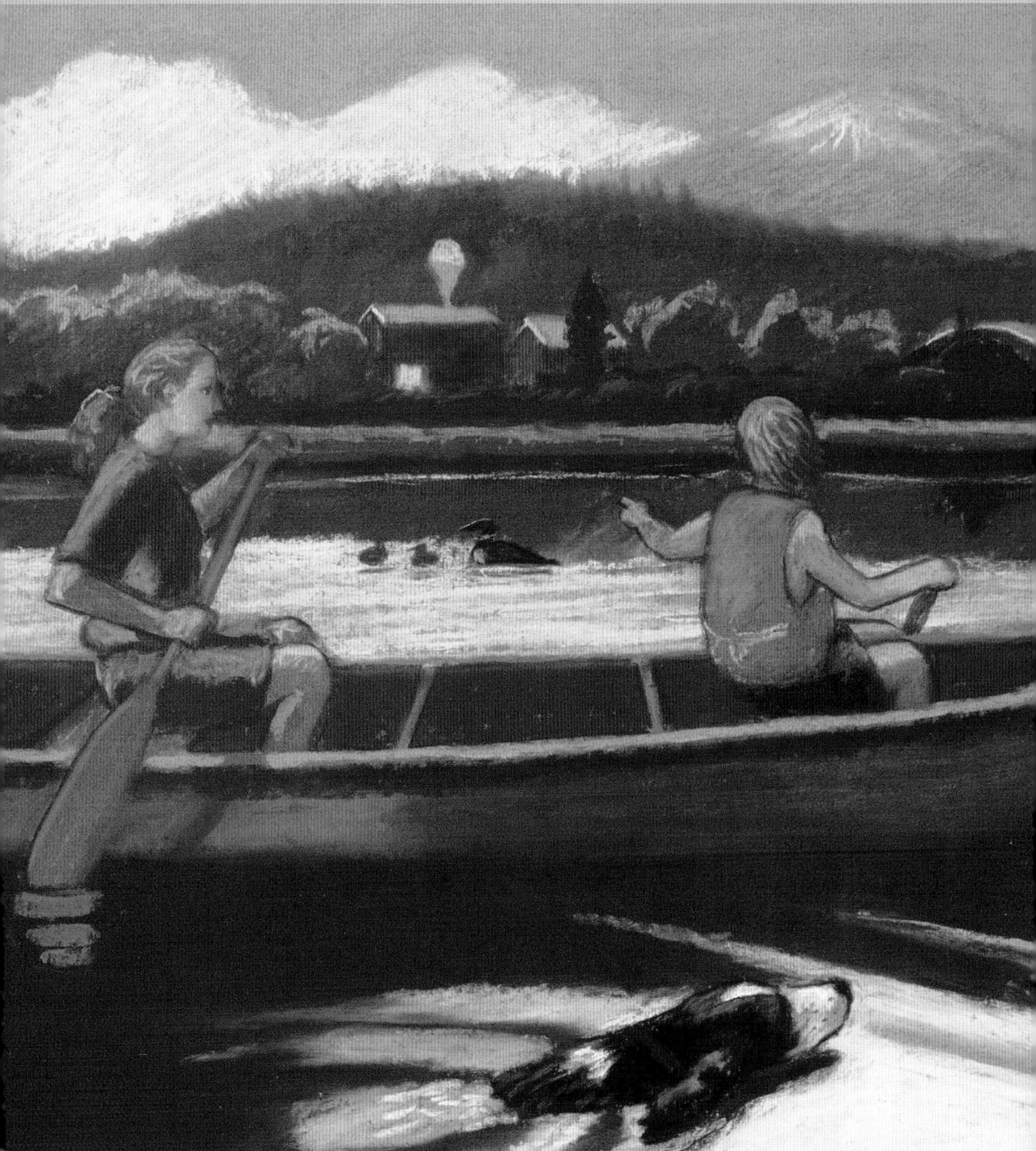

Miles loved to swim. He could dog-paddle faster than I could paddle a canoe.

I made a triangle with my arms and the neck of my wooden paddle, dipped the paddle into the lake, and pulled—just like Mom had taught me.

"Can I go out to the island by myself soon?" I asked.

Mom just smiled. I could tell that it wouldn't be long until she said, "yes."

At the end of the lake, by the mill, a loon and two loon chicks were swimming. Loons were rare birds, and seeing them was as exciting as watching a shooting star. There were so few left in the world, and it was against the law to hurt one. I was glad that they were far away, though. Miles was a bird dog; he wasn't mean, but he just had to chase every bird he saw.

"Pfuh-huh—pfuh-huh." His nose sprayed silvery drops. Luckily, Miles was too busy swimming to see the loons.

At Big Island, I stood in the canoe picking berries while Mom held the boat steady. Now we were busy, so we didn't notice when Miles stopped sniffing around in the bushes and swam away.

Sound carries a long way over water. Before we saw Miles again we heard, "Pfuh-huh—pfuh-huh, pfuh-huh—pfuh-huh." The sun bounced so brightly off the lake that we had to squint to see him, out in the middle, his black head pointed straight toward three tiny specks—the loons.

Loons Nesting
Please
Keep Away

I tossed the berries I had in my hand into the bucket. We jabbed our paddles onto the rocks to push off.

We had to stop him.

Miles was our family pet. He played ball, slept on a dog bed and ate out of a bowl, but when he saw a bird, something came over him. He had never been close to catching one in our yard. These loons were on the water though—and two of them were babies!

Mom canoed faster than ever. I started to paddle, but I got so scared Miles would catch a loon chick that I froze up and quit. While the boat raced along, I held my paddle on my lap like a useless stick. A dragonfly flew up and hovered over the blade.

"I need your help if we're going to head him off," Mom said. So I pushed at the dark water again. It felt as thick as chocolate icing.

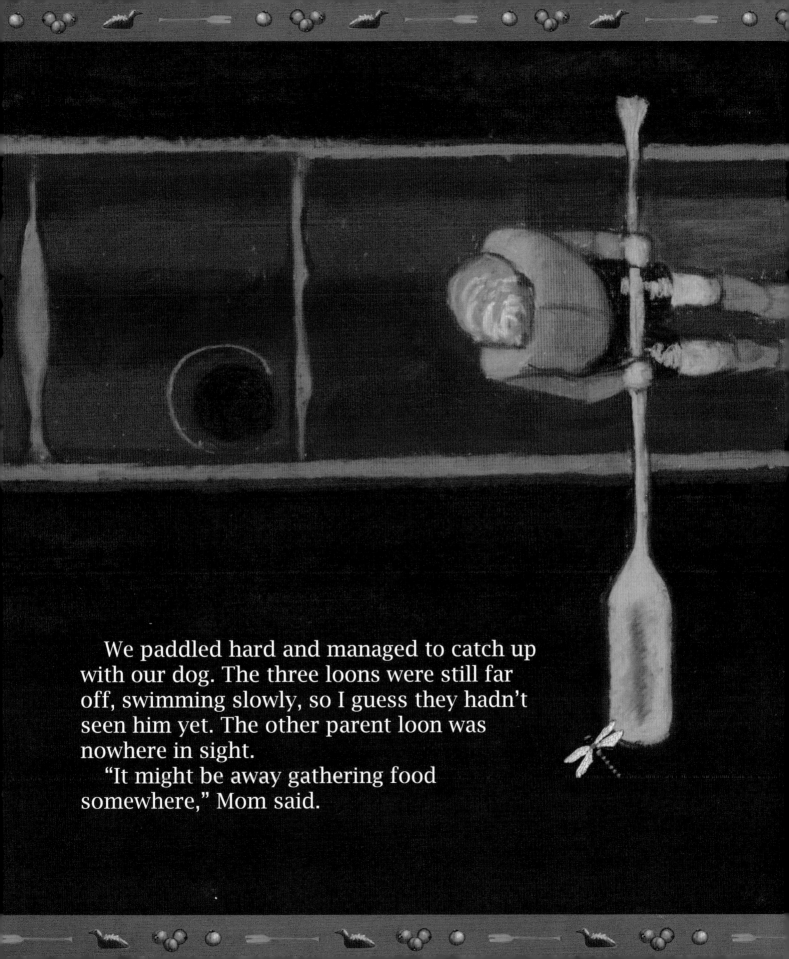

We paddled hard and managed to catch up with our dog. The three loons were still far off, swimming slowly, so I guess they hadn't seen him yet. The other parent loon was nowhere in sight.

"It might be away gathering food somewhere," Mom said.

She turned the canoe so it crossed Miles' path, but he swam around the boat. She tried prodding him with her paddle, to point him in a different direction. He ducked and came up near me at the bow. I reached out to grab his collar—and missed.

"Miles!" I yelled. He swam off.

"Get my paddle!" Mom shouted behind me. In the confusion, it had slipped from her hands.

I pushed and pulled with my paddle and somehow yanked the canoe close enough for Mom to reach in and grab hers. By the time we turned the boat back toward the loons, Miles had almost reached them.

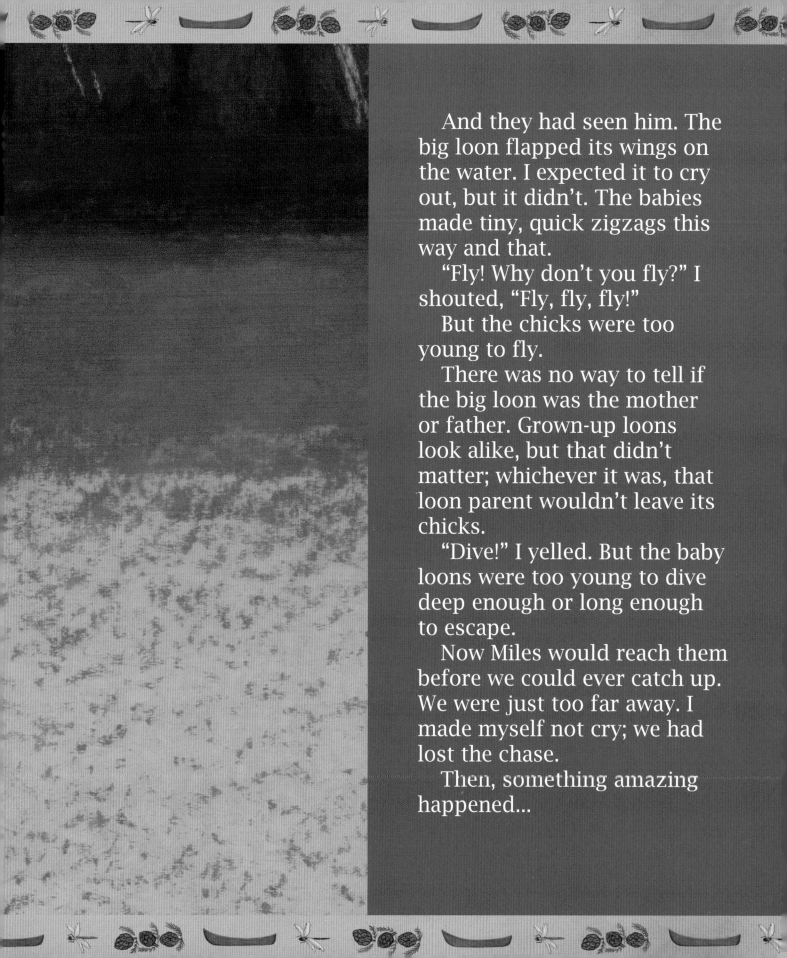

And they had seen him. The big loon flapped its wings on the water. I expected it to cry out, but it didn't. The babies made tiny, quick zigzags this way and that.

"Fly! Why don't you fly?" I shouted, "Fly, fly, fly!"

But the chicks were too young to fly.

There was no way to tell if the big loon was the mother or father. Grown-up loons look alike, but that didn't matter; whichever it was, that loon parent wouldn't leave its chicks.

"Dive!" I yelled. But the baby loons were too young to dive deep enough or long enough to escape.

Now Miles would reach them before we could ever catch up. We were just too far away. I made myself not cry; we had lost the chase.

Then, something amazing happened...

The big loon rose up in the water. It flapped its wings and splashed its webbed feet as though it were walking on the lake. Below, down in the water, the dog's head looked very small. The bird spread its huge wings between Miles and the babies. Its feet began to dance, faster and faster. Water flashed up in the sun and foamed white, like a fountain in the middle of the lake.

Whoosh—Miles lunged at the loon. The water splashed up even higher. What was happening?

Wait!

Miles was turning back.

He was swimming toward our canoe! That loon looked delicate and beautiful, but on the water it was fiercer than our dog.

The loon was swimming too—in the opposite direction, as if the dog were still chasing it. We couldn't see the chicks.

When Miles passed us, we could see that there was nothing in his mouth except bubbles. We followed him. He climbed out of the lake, shook off, and lay panting on the dock, "Heh-heh heh-heh heh-heh heh-heh."

Mom clipped the leash back onto his collar.

"I want to go out by myself and make sure the chicks are okay," I said.

She looked at me carefully.

"All right," she said. She would watch me and hold Miles.

I steered back to Big Island. Alone in the canoe for the first time, I wasn't scared, just disappointed not to find the loons on the other side of the island or in the cove.

From the dock, Mom waved and pointed to where we had picked blueberries.

There they were: two big loons now, and—yes—the two chicks between them.

I stopped paddling and let the canoe float. One of the parents dropped its head forward under the water and dove without a sound or a ripple.

A few inches from the canoe, it came up again. I heard nothing. It just appeared. It was so close to me that I could have reached out and touched it.

Well, I knew—I just instantly knew: this was the loon Miles had chased.

It was twice as big as it had looked from far away—bigger than any duck. The tip of its beak was thin and as sharp as the point of a knife. Its black was the deepest black; it's white, pure white. And, it looked like it was wearing a necklace. It was hard to believe that no one had painted that exact pattern on its feathers.

The loon looked at me with its red eye and did not move. Had it come up in this spot on purpose, or was the loon as surprised as I was?

We stared at each other, for what felt like several minutes. Then, just as silently as it had arrived, the bird again dove and was gone.

After dinner that night, Mom and I sat on the dock to look for shooting stars. At our feet, Miles lay curled up—fast asleep. When the loons cried out in the dark, he was too tired to hear them.

Mom and I listened. Those weird loon voices called to each other like sad laughter. Then one of the loons whisked through the moonlit air, close to the surface of the lake. It looked like a black bowling pin with a spear-shaped tip as it flew—out of the wild and back into the night.

Creative Minds
Loon Fun Facts

A loon is a large water bird that looks something like a duck, but is not related to a duck at all. Loons belong to a family of ancient birds, at least 20 million years old.

The best-known species is the common loon *(Gavia immer)*, which spends summers on lakes in the Northern United States and Canada. In winter, common loons live on the ocean along the Pacific coast, all the way to Mexico, and along the Atlantic coast, south to Florida and the Gulf of Mexico.

> *Look at a map and identify where Loons spend the summer and winter. Do they live in your area?*

The common loon is famous for the black and white pattern of its summer feathers, and its many eerie, unmistakable calls.

> *To hear loon calls, go to www.SylvanDellPublishing.com and click on "Loon Chase."*

Common loons weigh between 8 and 15 pounds and get larger in size as you go from west to east (Maine has larger loons compared to the west or Midwest.) They are 28 to 35 inches long with a wingspan of an adult being up to 58 inches wide.

> *Math activity: find something in the house or classroom that weighs 10 pounds (bags of flour, a few books). Use a yard stick to see how long a loon is and how wide the wingspan is. Use chalk to draw how big a loon is on the driveway, a quiet street, sidewalk, or playground.*

Scientists think loons may live as long as 30 years.

> *Who do you know who is about 30 years old? Does that seem old to you? Is that a long time for a bird?*

Male and female adult loons look alike, though the male is often a little bigger. Loons spend almost all of their lives on water, and come on land only to mate, build their nest, and to incubate their eggs.

While most birds have hollow, sponge-like bones, making their skeletons light, loons have solid bones. To lift their heavy bodies into the air, loons need a long runway, sometimes several hundred yards of water surface. Loons are able to fly at speeds of 60 to 90 miles per hour.

> *Many cars on a highway drive about 60 miles per hour. If a loon flies at 60 miles per hour, how long does it take to fly five miles? What is five miles from your house or school? How long does it take you to drive those five miles? Walk? Ride a bike?*

Underwater, loons almost always use their feet to move, not their wings.

What parts of your body do you use to swim?

Loons have been known to dive to depths of more than 100 feet. They usually dive for about a minute at a time to hunt for food.

How long can you hold your breath? How deep can you dive in a swimming pool?

Loons eat small fish, insects, snails, crayfish, frogs, and salamanders.

Loons migrate each season, flying back from their winter, ocean homes usually to the same lake. Loon pairs are territorial during the breeding season which means they defend an area around their nest and young, chasing other loons away if they come too close. Sometimes these chases lead to intense fights between the birds. Loons usually pair off with the same partner each year, but not always.

Loons' webbed feet (adapted for swimming) are set so far back on their bodies that it is difficult for them to walk on land.

They build their nests right at the shoreline because they need to slip on and off the nest without being seen by predators. Sometimes people will float an artificial nesting platform for a loon to nest on, which is especially useful on lakes where dams artificially raise or lower the water level each year.

After the female lays one or two olive-colored eggs, the male and female share the job of sitting on them until they hatch after 27-28 days. Chicks spend their first couple of hours drying off in the nest and then leave it forever. They move to the lake to swim. For the first two weeks, young chicks often ride on their parents' backs to rest and to be protected from eagles, large fish, and snapping turtles that may try to eat them. Loon parents keep their chicks in a sheltered "nursery" area of the lake until they are three to four weeks old. Their feathers turn from downy brown to gray, and gradually the young loons swim in a larger part of the lake.

In the fall, the adult loons leave the lake to return to the ocean before the young loons do. The adults also lose their black and white summer feathers, which are replaced by gray, winter plumage. Young loons are ready to fly when they are 10 to 12 weeks old. When they reach the ocean, they stay there for several years before returning to the lakes to breed.

The common loon is the state bird of Minnesota.

For further information and activities related to this book (Animal Instincts, Take a Bird Census Math Activity) and to find Loon-related internet links (including loon cams, migrations and listening to loon calls), please go to *www.SylvanDellPublishing.com* and click on *"Loon Chase."*

Loons in Native American Culture

For centuries, the common loon has captured people's imaginations and inspired stories. There are many references to loons in Native American culture, especially among the cultures of native peoples who inhabited the Arctic, Subartic, and Northwest Coast. This includes Greenland, Canada, and in the USA, both the Great Lakes region and the Pacific Northwest.

- In the Ojibwa language, the word 'mahng' means both 'brave' and 'loon.'

- Of the five great clans of the Ojibwa people, one was called the Loon Clan.

- If a loon was heard the night before a battle, this was considered a sign of good luck.

- The Cree connected the cry of the loon to the cry of dead warriors calling back to the land of the living.

- The Eskimo are said to have at least thirty different names for loons; the name used most often is 'Tuutlik.'

One of the best-known Native American loon tales emphasizes the bird's ability for diving and explains how it got the beautiful design of black and white feathers on its neck. In this story, a blind boy rides underwater on a loon's back for three long dives. After the third dive, the boy regains his sight and frees himself of an evil grandmother. In thanks, he gives the loon a shell necklace. With his newfound eyesight, he becomes a great hunter but never kills loons.

In another version of this story, a boy saves an injured loon and gives the necklace to the loon to help it heal. Later, the boy himself falls ill and, believing his people don't want him anymore, he crawls off to drown himself in a lake. The loon he saved rescues him. This loon turns out to be the chief of all loons. After four rides across the lake and underwater, hanging onto Loon Chief's back, the boy is cured. Loon Chief teaches the boy to be a shaman – a great healer and wise man – who then returns to help his people.

Make a Loon Mask

You can make a ceremonial loon mask, like one used by the Yup'ik (Eskimo) people. Centuries ago, masks like this one may have been used to express a desire for good luck before a hunt. The fish in the loon's mouth may have symbolized a hunter's wish to find plenty of food for his people.

The design for this project was inspired by a Yup'ik (Eskimo) mask.

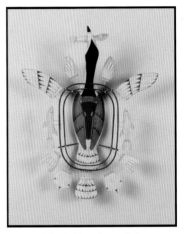

Yup'ik (Eskimo) mask by
Edward Kiokun, about 1981:
Courtesy, National Museum
of the American Indian,
Smithsonian Institution.

Supplies needed:

White, black, and
 green construction paper
One red sequin
Pipe cleaners
Tooth picks
Popsicle stick
Glue stick
Hot glue gun or craft glue

Yup'ik Loon Mask Craft you
can make using cut paper and
pipe cleaners.

· Copy or download the patterns from *www.SylvanDellPublishing.com*.

· Cut out the patterns.

· Place the patterns onto the colored construction paper and trace around them.

· Cut out the paper pieces.

· Using a glue stick, glue the black beak, neck, and wings onto the white body of the loon. Glue the red sequin on to the loon's head as the eye and glue one fish under the loon's beak.

· Twist the pipe cleaners into two ovals. One oval should be slightly larger than the other. Cut some pipe cleaners into 3" pieces. Using these short pieces, attach the ovals to each other in several places.

· With the hot glue gun or craft glue, attach the toothpicks to the back of the fish and feather pieces. Then glue the entire loon body onto the center of the pipe cleaner oval.

· With the hot glue gun or craft glue, attach the tooth pick ends of the feather and fish pieces onto the pipe cleaners.

· Glue the popsicle stick to the back of the loon, at the bottom of the toothpick oval. (A glue gun works best).

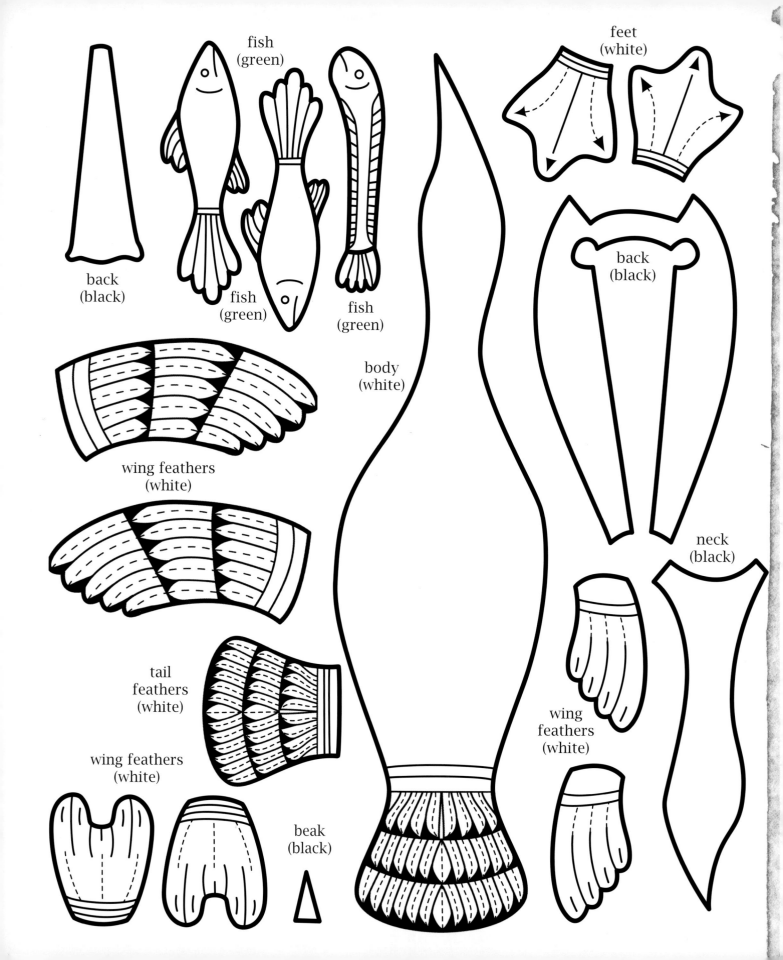

back
(black)

fish
(green)

fish
(green)

fish
(green)

wing feathers
(white)

body
(white)

feet
(white)

back
(black)

neck
(black)

tail
feathers
(white)

wing
feathers
(white)

wing feathers
(white)

beak
(black)